My Mud Puddle Ran Away

Copyright © 1998 by Valerie Mazza
and Jeremy Vanisacker, First Edition

Proctor Publications, LLC
PO Box 2498
Ann Arbor, MI 48106–2498
(800) 343-3034

Written by VALERIE L. MAZZA

Illustrated by JEREMY VANISACKER

Publisher's Cataloging-in-Publication
(Provided by Quality Books, Inc.)

Mazza, Valerie L.
   My mud puddle ran away / written by Valerie L. Mazza ;
illustrated by Jeremy Vanisacker. -- 1st ed.
   p. cm.
   Preassigned LCCN: 98-66127
   ISBN: 1-882792-63-7
   SUMMARY: A young boy who likes to play in a mud puddle is
sad when it disappears, until his mother explains that rainy
weather will restore the puddle in due season.
   1. Mud--Juvenile fiction. 2. Rain and rainfall--Juvenile
fiction. 3. Seasons--Juvenile fiction.   I. Vanisacker,
Jeremy. II. Title.

PZ7.M474My 1998   [E]
                      QBI98-784

Printed in USA

S0-DOP-382

For all the children who have touched my life, especially,
Krista, Mike, and Tracy.
VLM

To my sister Jessica, and my brother Brandon.
JPV

Special thanks to Janet MacDonald

I was awakened one Sunday morning from the rain beating against the roof and my bedroom window.

1.

The rain was coming down like cats and dogs.

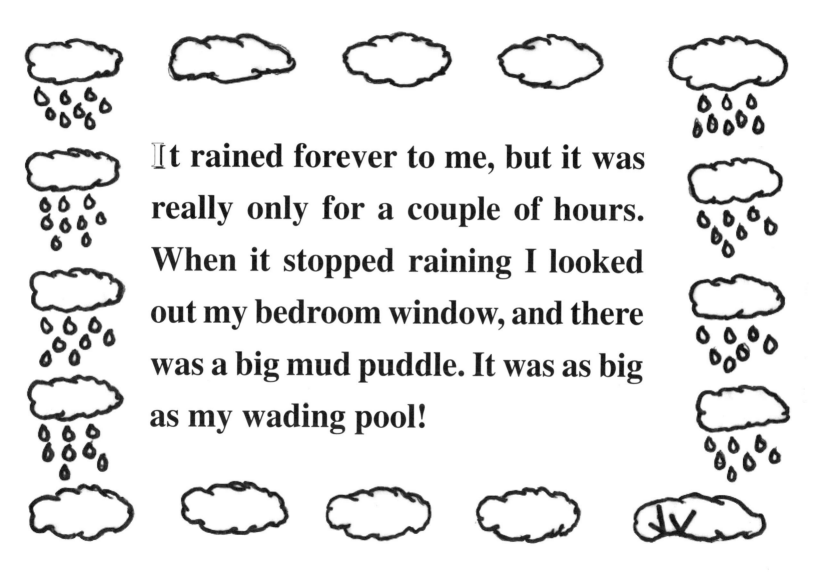

It rained forever to me, but it was really only for a couple of hours. When it stopped raining I looked out my bedroom window, and there was a big mud puddle. It was as big as my wading pool!

As fast as I could, I put on my swimming trunks. I was going to go swimming in MY puddle!

But guess who stopped me on the way out the door? Yep, you're right. Mom said, "No swimming in the mud." But she did say that I could go wading in my mud puddle.

So, I quickly put on my clothes and rolled up my jeans so I could go wading.

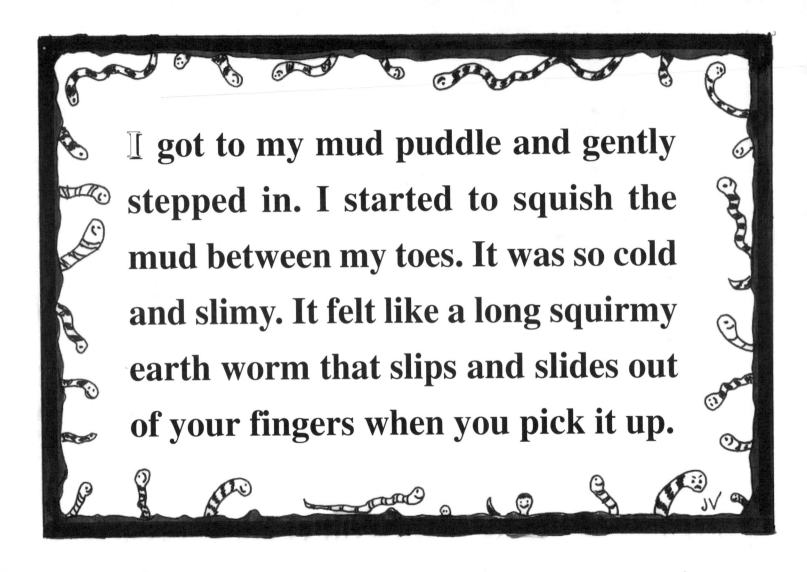

I got to my mud puddle and gently stepped in. I started to squish the mud between my toes. It was so cold and slimy. It felt like a long squirmy earth worm that slips and slides out of your fingers when you pick it up.

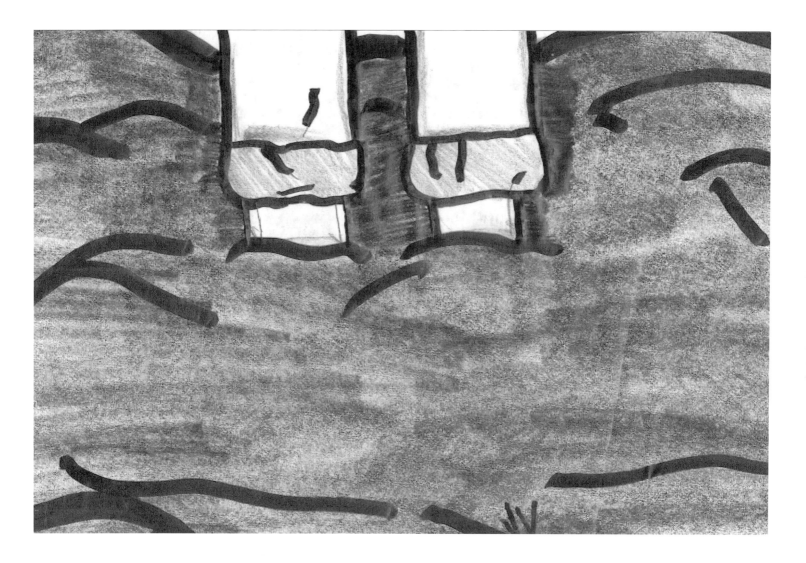

I knew the puddle liked me because it started to bubble and gurgle, kind of like how a kitten purrs when it likes you.

11.

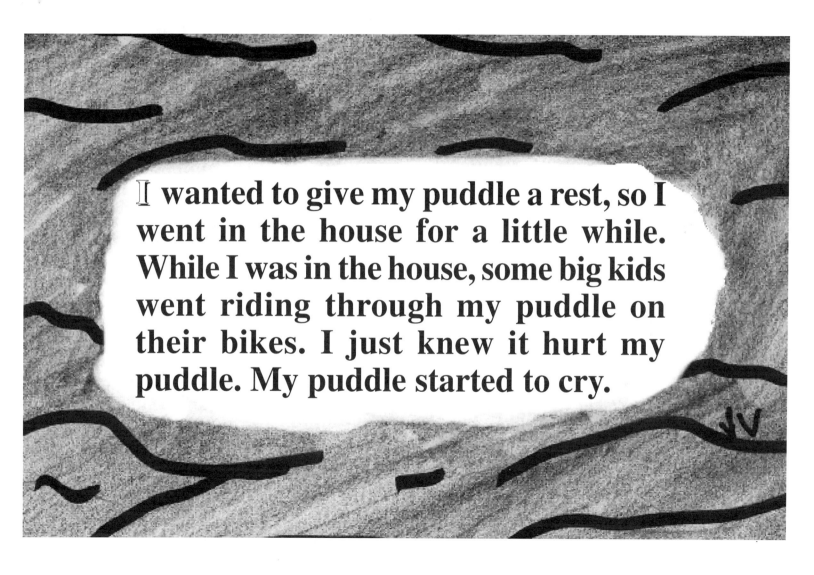

I wanted to give my puddle a rest, so I went in the house for a little while. While I was in the house, some big kids went riding through my puddle on their bikes. I just knew it hurt my puddle. My puddle started to cry.

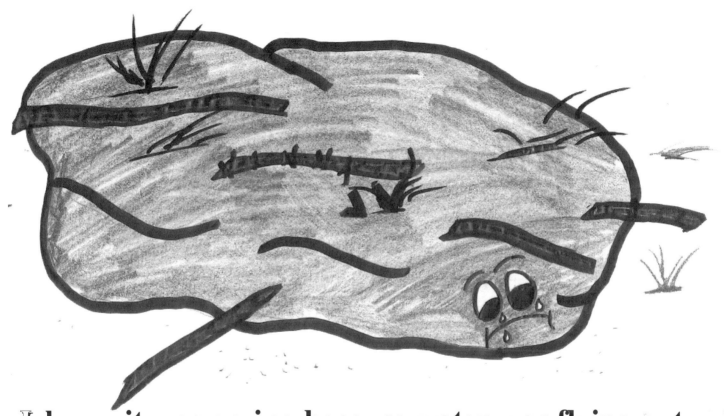

I knew it was crying because water was flying out,
and it had a deep crease on its bottom. I just knew
that my puddle was hurt.

I ran out to my puddle and smoothed it out again.
I rubbed the bottom of it for a little while. It bubbled
and gurgled again. I knew it liked me.

15.

It was getting late, so I went to bed. While I was sleeping, I had dreams about everything I would do with my puddle after school tomorrow.

16.

The next morning I woke up and got ready
for school. As I went to the bus stop, kids with
boots on were stomping in my mud puddle.

17.

When I came home from school, I was really
excited. I could finally play with my puddle.
But when I got home my mud puddle was gone! 18.

I ran into the house crying. I told my mom that my mud puddle ran away because those big kids hurt it with their bikes and boots.

19.

My mom said I was wrong. She said my mud puddle went away because the sun came out and dried up my mud puddle. But she promised when it rains again my puddle will come back.

20.

21.

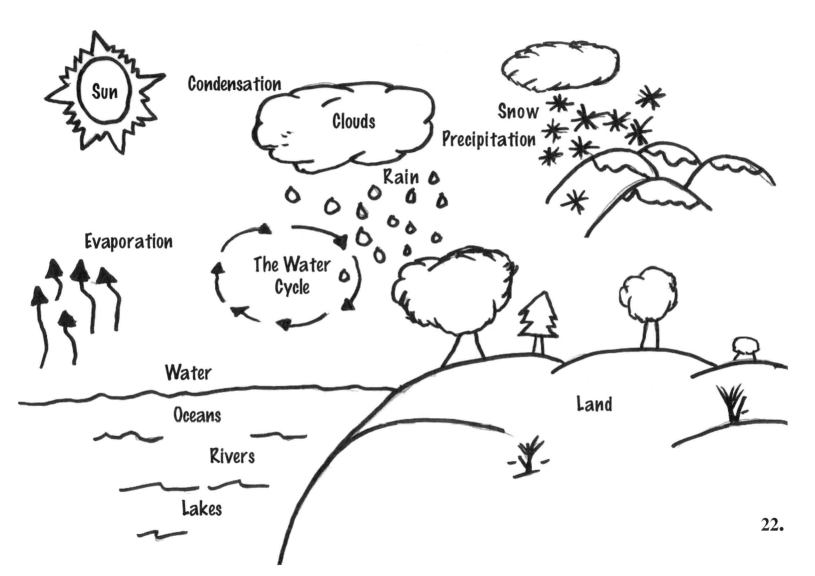

Sun

Condensation

Clouds

Snow

Precipitation

Rain

Evaporation

The Water Cycle

Water

Oceans

Rivers

Lakes

Land

22.

About the Author

Valerie Mazza is an elementary school teacher at Smith Road Elementary in Temperance, Michigan. She is married and has two daughers and a son. She received her bachelor's degree from Siena Heights College and is currently working toward a master's degree in reading. In her spare time, she enjoys walking, reading and bike riding. Her goal as an educator is to guide her students to their maximum potential and to constantly remind them how valuable and precious they are.

About the Illustrator

Jeremy P. Vanisacker is a high school honors student who enjoys drawing in his spare time, and also plays for his high school football and basketball teams. One of his many goals is to become a lawyer as he plans to study prelaw after he graduates in 2001.

Jeremy, thank you for for all of your hard work on this book.

Love,
    Aunt Valerie